Pearl
The Promise

by

Baaron Lōc Mogul

Edited by Christal Nance

Dorrance Publishing Co
585 Alpha Drive
Suite 103
Pittsburgh, PA 15238
Visit our website at *www.dorrancebookstore.com*

ISBN: 979-8-8852-7181-3
eISBN: 979-8-8852-7637-5

Pearl
The Promise

by

Baaron Lōc Mogul

Edited by **Christal Nance**

Contents

Chapter 1
Mustang

The events in this book are all true, and although they happened a long time ago, I am writing them down the best I can remember.

This was a time before everyone had cell phones and internet. If you had a pager, you were at the top of the digital age. Sure, some people had cell phones, but not in my circle. They weighed around five pounds and cost $1,000. I do remember this day, and I remember it so vividly. Times were simpler, and people paid more attention to other people than to screens. They spent more time enjoying the outdoors and experiencing life rather than watching all of that on their phones and pads.

I was driving a 1966 orange convertible Mustang with a white interior, anyone's dream car. I was carefree and wasn't going anywhere in particular. With no mission in mind, I was just driving in the beautiful weather—the kind of weather people write about in fiction novels. At the time, I didn't know where I was. The sun was beaming down, gracing me with its natural warmth. The top was down on the convertible, and I let my long, moppy blonde hair blow around. The road was winding with turns I took just because I could, and I kept at a reasonable speed, so I wouldn't find myself in a ditch.

I didn't care where I was because I was having the time of my life. The trees were blowing in the mild breeze, and I could see the leaves that canopied the road. Farm fields were plentiful and showed in straight rows of corn and soybeans. A large creek to my right meandered through the countryside, in and out of my sight. I hadn't seen a house or building for a long time and made a mental note of how strange that seemed. No other cars shared the road with me, and no people were around.

I did think I was pretty cool; a handsome young man with my long, curly locks blowing in the wind in this incredible car. That seemed to make up for the strange desolation that surrounded me. I thought I was something else—a real ladies' man. It's such a funny thought now that I'm older and looking back on those days.

Now I noticed the creek to my right once again, and I slowed down to turn on a road toward it. Up ahead, I saw something no one should ever see—a life altering image. To this day, it sticks in my mind like a photograph I just can't forget. I had to rub my eyes open and close repeatedly to erase what I was sure was an illusion. The bright sun was playing tricks with my eyes. This couldn't be happening; I couldn't be seeing this. I was just out for a cruise, and I didn't want any trouble or circumstances that I had to be involved in.

Again the thought of where I was came into my mind, this time as an alarm. Where could I be that such a sight would appear before me? Now I had even more questions. Where did I get this car? It wasn't mine. Why was I in the middle of nowhere with no civilization around? Except these two silhouettes in front of me…

Everything was wrong. As I got closer, I saw two children waving their arms back and forth to get my attention. I had a feeling none of this was a dream or real; it was something else. I pulled up to the children, and I could see them clearly now. They were blackened and decomposing with flesh flapping in the wind. Their hair was clumped and burned black from fire. Their eyeballs were dried up. They approached my car while holding hands.

Chapter 2
The Children

At this point, I know I should have been terrified, repulsed, sick…something. But those feelings didn't come. Instead, I was concerned, and I couldn't help but to look at them with love. I didn't pay any attention to how horrid their appearance was because I wanted to help them. They were just little children.

The taller child was a boy who was probably around 10 or 11 years old. The smaller child was a girl who couldn't have been older than seven. I don't know how I know this, but they had to be siblings. The boy showed his protectiveness over his sister by holding on to her hand without fail. They seemed like two people who were molded together.

As I got out of the car, I knelt to their level and asked what happened to them. The boy replied with a shaky voice, "Can you help us?"

The girl spoke up before I could answer.

"We haven't seen anyone in a long, long time, and we may never see anyone again." Her voice was soft and innocent.

I felt pure concern and compassion as I looked at them. Who would do such a thing to these children? The horrible shells of human bodies they were occupying didn't deter me from wanting to help them any way I could. I told them both to get into the car.

The boy spoke and told me their names, but for some reason, I can't remember them. I have tried and tried to remember the names. I just can't. This has bothered me for years. I still feel bad for not remembering.

I said, "Come on, kids, and get in the car. I'll take you to get help."

I was thinking about how I didn't even know where I was or what I would say once I got to someone who could help. People might run or get sick when they saw how those kids looked, or they might wonder what I've done to them. I didn't want the kids to get their feelings hurt. They were just children and needed help. No one better say or do anything to hurt these kids again. They had been through enough. Looking back, I realize my feelings were paternal. I was their guardian that day.

The boy looked at me with charred eyes and said, "We can't get in your car. We are over there." He pointed his index finger to a grassy area overgrown with weeds off the road. I couldn't help but notice his hand was burnt with flesh hanging off the bone. His sister took my hand.

I wish I could remember their names, and I tire of calling them the kids, little children, boy or girl. However, I don't want to make up names because this is a true story. Making up names for them might hinder further investigation into if these kids existed and what happened to them. I believe with my whole heart that they once lived, and they want to be found.

As the little girl took my hand, I knelt so I could be face to face with her. Her brother stood a few feet away and looked at her with love and concern. He obviously wanted nothing more than to protect her. Perhaps there was guilt in his gaze as well because of how everything turned out.

She said, "We can't go with you. You have to bring help. We are over there." Her finger pointed exactly where her brother pointed moments earlier. She was a smart little girl, and I think her hair was once blonde, but it was hard to tell with the black clumps and singed color.

I could smell the burnt aroma around both kids. It would have made my stomach turn if I hadn't wanted so badly to help them. That feeling easily overtook the nausea. The grassy area they both pointed to had weeds scattered throughout.

I looked at the field and didn't understand at the time what they meant. The ground looked settled and like it hadn't been disturbed in quite a while.

"They were over there, and they can't go. Come on," said the little girl as she took my hand again. Her brother took my other hand as they led me across the tar and seal road to the overgrown field between the farmers' crop fields. I imagined this could have once been where a homestead was, and as we got further off the road, I noticed what appeared to be something that looked like an old chimney. It was hidden from the road and was half fallen in and only a couple of feet off of the ground. Then I noticed that the underbrush covered the entire concrete slab of what used to be a foundation. It was difficult to see without pushing the weeds to the side.

Chapter 3
The Cellar

As I walked toward the foundation, I noticed what appeared to be a broken and eroded slab. Nature had tried to take the field back, but the concrete wasn't ready to let go yet. I started kicking at the debris and the weeds to get a better look at what the concrete was hiding. Beneath the slab was burnt wood and gravel. I was sure now that this was once where a house stood.

The boy said, "This is where we live."

I looked around the vacant lot and realized the house that once stood here must have burned down long ago. Several small trees had started to grow up through the cracked foundation. I walked around the perimeter of where the house had stood and began rummaging through the debris. I don't know what I was looking for. Maybe I wanted to find clues of who these kids were or what happened to them so long ago. I had so many questions that needed answered.

The slab of foundation where the chimney was sticking out was blackened by fire. As I looked past the chimney, I saw a creek running fast and loud enough for me to hear from where I stood. It must have emptied into a river further down. I couldn't help but picture the home. The greenery and the creek would have been a beautiful backdrop to a family home. Kids would have played outside for hours, entering the house only when their parents told them it was mealtime or bedtime. Surely there had been happy memories here.

The weather was still beautiful, even with the tone of the day becoming so mysterious. As I stood amongst the ruins of the burnt, debris-laden, overgrown field, I looked up at the beautiful trees swaying in the wind. I wish they could tell me what happened. The foundation stood as if it wanted to give answers. It wasn't ready to disappear yet.

I again held the hands of the little corpse children. At this point, I'm sure that seems crazy. How could this be a true story? I can assure you that you will understand, and it is true. It will make sense, and you might already be understanding just what is happening already.

About this time, the little girl started tugging at my shirt.

"Come over here," she said.

Her brother let go of my hand and stayed behind, kneeling on the foundation and playing with some of the burnt wood. He looked lost in thought. Maybe he was remembering playing with his toys long ago on that floor before it became a bare foundation. Maybe he still plays there every day.

The girl led me to the side of the burnt slab and pointed to a lot of debris stacked with vegetation growing over the top.

What shown was what appeared to be a few burnt and broken wood beams.

"My brother and I are down there," she said.

I looked over at her brother, and he was still kneeling down, fidgeting in the debris and gravel. It was as though he didn't want to acknowledge where his sister was pointing, almost looking afraid and shy. He was definitely avoiding participating in the conversation anymore. At this time, I reached down and grabbed at the overgrown vegetation and began tugging at it in handfuls. The plants were viny and hard to clear out.

Once I got most of the overgrowth pulled out of the way, I moved a few of the burnt beams and unstacked them. Beneath the stack, I found wooden double doors. I remembered seeing doors like these before. They were cellar doors, the kind that revealed stairs to a basement or cellar. The handles were made of metal but had been discolored from the fire and rainwater that rusted it.

The little girl moved closer and grabbed my hand again. She whispered, "We are down there," as if not wanting for her brother to hear.

I looked back at him, and his back was to us. He remained in place and didn't acknowledge us. I looked ahead of us, distracting myself with what I might find down the stone stairs. The river was beautiful, I thought to myself, not wanting to go down the dark, damp steps. They were cracked and covered in debris. I knew I had to, but I remember being scared. This dreadful nightmare's circumstance I was in was starting to make some sense to me now.

The little girl spoke again and brought me back to the steps in front of us.

"You don't have to go down there if you're scared to." She was such a brave child, and I found myself wanting to be brave for her. I did have to go down the steps, and I moved cautiously toward the first step. At this point, the little girl had let go of my hand and said, "We don't go down there."

I put my foot on the first step and thought to myself, *What am I doing here? How did this happen to me?* I was driving a 1966 orange convertible Mustang, top down, hair blowing in the wind, jamming to Boston's "Don't Look Back." It was a perfect day, cruising the country. I thought I was some kind of stud in that car on my way to who knows where, but not here. Now I was holding hands with and talking to corpses while exploring abandoned cellars out in the middle of nowhere. I literally didn't even know where.

Even with my brain running through how I possibly could have ended up here, I knew these kids needed my help. I went down the stairs. Darkness swallowed me, and the air was damp. An overwhelming scent assaulted my nostrils, and I didn't want to think what could cause such a smell. I went down one step, two steps, three steps…

After even just a few steps, I was alarmed at just how dark it was. I couldn't even see the floor or where the steps ended. Looking back, a flashlight or a modern-day cell phone would

have helped. I was a smoker then, so I grabbed my lighter and flicked it on. The flame sent a flickering light far enough to see at least a few feet in front of me. I held it up in front of me and continued the journey down the damp stairs.

Seven steps, eight steps… I don't remember how many stairs there were in all, but it felt like an hour passed when it was probably just seconds.

A flickering flame can be tricky. I couldn't look directly at the lighter because I would be blinded for a second and wouldn't be able to see past my hand. Instead, I looked past the lighter and made my way down to the bottom of the stairs, finally.

Upon reaching the bottom, I looked back up to where the cellar doors were open. It was amazing to me that I could only see a few steps at the top before the darkness overtook the sunlight. The little girl was gone, and I wondered how I even made it down safely. It was odd how there was absolutely no light down here from the surface. The lighter was getting hot, and I knew in a moment, I would be in total darkness. I had to give the lighter a break and let it cool down before I could use it again.

My thoughts were again taking over as I stood in the darkness, alone. Why did I stop the car? What was I thinking? If I had kept driving, I wouldn't be standing in an abandoned cellar where it smelled, was pitch black, and 400 yards or more off a road that leads to lost.

I imagined for a moment where the road could have taken me. I could have found a town and stopped at the police department. A trained police officer could have handled this situation better. The song by Boston was back in my mind, and I thought that the title could be prophetic. Maybe if I hadn't looked back, I would have found a little bar up the road. I could have stepped in and had a beer served up ice cold. But no. I stopped like an idiot and got involved in this nightmare. The only way to get out of this nightmare, though, was through it.

I stood in the total darkness, contemplating screaming. I still waited for the lighter to cool off. Part of me didn't want to see what was down there, and the other part was just scared of the pitch blackness.

When I flicked the lighter back on, I stumbled around the mess. I was barely able to see a few feet in front of me. As I walked around, I noticed an old wooden chair and some wooden crates on the floor. The fire had spared these somehow. The floor was mostly dry with only a few small puddles scattered in spaces.

I wanted to leave and go back to the beautiful sun-filled sky above. The stench was almost unbearable, and it was getting harder to breathe. My lighter was once again hot, so I had to let it cool again. The darkness enveloped me for a second time.

While standing in the darkness, I heard the little girl break the silence. She looked down the stairs but wouldn't touch them. Her sudden words scared the shit out of me, as my mind was racing, and I was done with this cellar for now. She said, "Are you okay?"

I acted like there was nothing to be afraid of and answered, "Yes."

I walked toward the stairs and understood for the first time what was really happening. I flicked my lighter to guide me up the stairs and moved quickly to the surface. On the floor beyond two broken crates, I noticed a picture frame that I missed on my descent. It looked old and worn, yellowed with age.

The damp smell of the cellar burned my nose. I covered my nose with my shirt and let the lighter turn off again. I decided to wait until I could use the lighter again to reach the frame. For now, I was swallowed by darkness and wanted to reach the surface again.

As I was standing near the stairs, I looked up and asked the girl, "Is your brother still with us?" I wanted to know that he was safe, but I also wanted to comfort myself while I was in the dark. Its blackness was beginning to overwhelm me.

She answered so quietly that I almost didn't hear her.

"Yes. He is playing with rocks." Her voice was comforting, even if she was a corpse.

Chapter 4
The Picture

Flick. Flick. A circle of light showed in front of me again as I turned on the lighter. Before I ascended the stairs, I looked at the picture frame in the debris. I didn't want to wait anymore and needed answers. I moved through the trash and debris. Fear climbed up my spine as I reached down for the frame. I grasped it and lifted it up, moving the lighter closer, so I could see the picture more clearly. The picture was black and white and showed a family. A man, woman, and two babies who were around two and four years old, smiling at the camera. They were all sitting on the porch swing of what looked like a beautiful home. I wondered if I was standing in the cellar of that very home now. The man and woman were handsome and looked happy. The woman was holding the youngest child while the older child, a boy, was holding the hand of the man I assumed to be his father while sitting on his lap. Questions filled my mind. Who was this family? Where were they now? Who took the picture? I decided to leave the picture and go back to the children. The idea of taking even the picture out of the cellar made me uncomfortable.

I made my way quickly up the stairs. The lighter was getting hot again, but I didn't want to let the light go out. I let the heat burn my finger until I reached the sunlight.

The little girl came right to me and took my hand. We closed the cellar doors together, as if we were closing the memories. The boy came running toward me like my trip to the cellar hadn't happened. I have a strong feeling he didn't want to talk about the situation or even see the cellar doors. He was once again engaged in what his sister and I were doing now that we were walking away from the closed doors. One corpse child held each of my hands, and we looked up at the deep blue sky and lush, green trees; still not a bird to be heard or seen.

This is the moment I knew two things. First, the young children in the picture were these children. Second, the bodies of these children had to be in that basement. My gut hinted that while I had been down there, but I was scared to find them. Now here I was talking to and holding the hands of their spirits.

Chapter 5
Jackson

Back from the darkness and to the light of day, I gazed at the beautiful water. I could hear water moving through rapids. We walked toward the sound. Beautiful sun, great, puffy clouds dispersed. Having my back turned to the cellar somehow soothed me. We stood together and gazed at the creek. A small, wooden canoe floated effortlessly on the placid water, and a white haired elderly man with a long white beard sat in it. He was navigating his way back to the shoreline. The kids let go of my hand and ran toward the old timer yelling, "Jackson!" excitedly.

The man, Jackson, I assume, got out of the canoe and smiled at the children. His eyes were kind, and his aged face radiated wisdom. He said, "Children! How wonderful to see you!" They each took one of his hands as soon as he finished tying his canoe to a small tree. The kids guided him toward me.

One child stood on each side of him, and his large hands gently held each child's burnt hand. They were smiling and chatting, and I knew they must see Jackson as a grandfather figure. As he approached me, it was clear that he knew them well. He wasn't alarmed by their appearance, and I couldn't help but wonder why he hadn't helped the children.

"Good day, young man," Jackson said with a smile. He let go of the little girl's hand to shake mine. I shook his hand firmly but could hardly smile. I returned the greeting.

"Glad to meet you, Jackson." We walked back to the remnants of the house. My mind went back to the kids: *I'm spending too much time here, and these kids need help.* I was straight to the point and said just that to Jackson. "Let's go and get help for these kids."

I didn't expect Jackson's response.

"They have help now, Neil. That's why they stopped you. Not everyone can find us. That's why when they saw you, they ran toward you. They knew you would stop. Remember, it's been a long time since they have even seen anyone, and they have been looking for someone like you."

How does he know my name? And what does he mean by "us"?

At the time, a lot of what was going on wasn't making any sense to me, but looking back, I see it for what it was. It's much clearer now. I'm a straight shooter and always have been. I said, "Jackson, what did you have in mind?"

"Neil, take my canoe downstream, navigate the waters carefully, and when you get to the next town, you will know exactly what to do. I will stay with the children for a while. I check up on them when they need me, so I will be here with them."

At this time, so much was going through my head. Like why would I take a canoe down a creek by myself? It's so slow, and I'm not a man who spends a lot of time in nature. If I want to get somewhere, I walk or drive. Why would I use a canoe if I have an amazing '66 convertible Mustang up there on the road?

The little girl ran to me, hugged me, and said, "When I saw you, I knew you would help us. Please don't forget us. Please."

Her brother joined her and hugged me as well. He said, "Thank you for stopping. My sister is smart, and she was right. You stopped. No one has stopped for a long time, and you have given my little sister hope. Please hurry back, and please, please don't forget us. We will be here waiting for you."

I hugged them both. I couldn't help but love these two kids, so it was difficult to say goodbye to them.

Jackson said, "It takes a special person to do what you have done. Now go and finish this." He shook my hand and continued, "Don't forget us, Neil. You must hurry because nightfall is coming. Navigating that creek at night is very dangerous."

Walking down the slope toward the creek, I heard little voices saying:

"Be careful."

"Bye, Neil."

"Hurry back. We will be waiting."

My thoughts were all over the place. Instead of questioning any of these people, I accepted what I had to do. This was crazy. I turned and got one last look at the three of them standing next to the old, collapsed chimney. I gave them a last wave and said I would get help and would be back. I don't even know why I said that when I wasn't even sure where I was or how to get back.

My mind was going crazy, thinking of what I had just witnessed. Even so, I went off and untied the canoe from the tree. I pushed it into the water and waded through it. I could feel the water soaking my shoes and pants, thinking how good the cool water felt as I climbed into the canoe. It was a hot day, and the water was refreshing.

Chapter 6
The Trip

The water was swift and helped me move downstream with ease. I couldn't help thinking about how odd Jackson had been. He seemed so wise, and I think he was wearing a robe. I hadn't thought to notice that while I spoke to him. And how did he know my name? I wondered how old he was. His face was kind, his eyes bright, and his hair was pure white. He was obviously elderly, but he moved with ease. Where had he come from? He came from one direction, but why did he tell me to go the opposite way downstream?

I splashed some of the cool water on me from time to time to control the heat that sank into my body. I gazed around at the beautiful landscape, noticing the trees on either side of the creek and how big and plentiful they were. I also looked at the crystal clear water. I could see the bottom of the creek bed and thought to myself, *It must be 10-12 feet deep...* I'd never seen a creek so deep and clear. When I fished in a creek as a boy, I could never see the bottom. Dirt, branches, and creek debris always muddied the water. This water was different. I caught myself wondering how I ended up reminiscing about my childhood and fishing after what I saw with the corpse kids. I looked around me and noticed that I still hadn't seen a single house, car, building, or person. I had traveled some distance by now.

Another strange observation is that I hadn't seen an animal, fish, or bug. I hadn't even seen a bird, which was odd with all these trees and fields. I hadn't so much as heard a bird.

After paddling for a long time, my arms were getting tired and sore. The sun was starting to set, and I wondered if I would ever find anyone. Or would I find more ghosts? Is that what they were? What about the elderly man?

Did this really happen to me? It seemed like I had been trapped in this land of desolation for days. I started to panic. I had to find a way out. What if I'm trapped here, too? Did I crash that Mustang somewhere up there and join the land of ghosts?

I should have taken the car. Plain and simple. I wouldn't have been in that mess if I had taken the Mustang. For that matter, I should never have stopped. I'm sure I would have been in some random town having a beer and talking to actual people, playing pool or something. I wanted out of there, and I was getting desperate.

I was on the verge of a panic attack when I saw a sign in the distance on the side of the shoreline. I looked at it as I got closer. The sign was weathered and beaten up. I could decipher the name on the sign: Pearl.

Chapter 7

Back from the Land of the Dead

Bam! My cat, Tibby, jumped on my chest and woke me up, scaring me so badly that I jumped and let out a yelp. Last I remembered, I had just splashed myself with the creek water to cool off from the heat of the late day and was in that stupid canoe in God knows where. "Pearl," the sign had said. I could see it clearly. The sign was green with white letters, looking old with paint chipped.

What a dream! It seemed so real to me. I had never had a vision before, so I wasn't sure if that was what it was. But I couldn't get over how real it was. If Tibby hadn't jumped on me while I was sleeping, what would have happened?

This turned out to be just the beginning. I wasn't done with that dream yet, and it wasn't done with me either.

I laid there petting Tibby and thought about everything that had happened. I wrote everything down about the kids, the car, Jackson, the creek, the cellar…that cellar. I didn't want to think about that part. I know I loved the kids, and I had the feeling of heartache and abandonment. *Wait a minute,* I thought. I jumped up and looked out of the window, down at the parking lot, looking for the '66 orange Mustang. I thought, just for a moment, it might be parked out there. The dream had to be real. It felt so real. I kept thinking about it, feeling a bit lost and unsure of what to do. Are the kids alright? What do I do?

I decided to call my friend, Walker, and tell him about it. Maybe he would know about visions, because that's what I thought this was. I just needed to verify this and get another opinion. Now, I can tell you, I have had plenty of dreams in my life, but I never had one that I took action over. None seemed as real and desperate as this one.

As I looked out the window for the car, I decided to check my shoes. If they were wet, this could have really happened. It may not have been a dream. The parking lot was dark, and I couldn't see the car. The shoes were also dry. I knew when I called my friend and asked him about visions and dreams, he would think I was crazy. But that's what I did. I told him everything: the burned children, the cellar, Jackson, the creek, and the sign "Pearl."

After telling Walker everything, he said maybe it really was a vision. Maybe there were some ghosts out there who contacted me and were waiting for me to come back. He was supportive and added another possibility with a laugh: "And maybe you're crazy."

Walker was my best friend and had been for 15 years. We had done some crazy things together, and he had the same sense of humor as me. That's why he was my best friend. We both liked pranking people to get a response, usually a bewildered one. I remember we both dated some very questionable girls, who happened to be friends. An acquaintance had mentioned to Walker and me at a party that, "You guys are dating the worst girls in town."

I gave a relaxed, "Really? Cool," response. Walker and I looked at each other and burst into laughter. The acquaintance hadn't expected my response and was disgusted. He walked away as Walker and I continued laughing.

Walker caught his breath and said, "We win!" We just found out we were dating the worst girls in town and acted like we had just won a seven door prize. That's just how we both are; always pushing for that response.

I got off the phone with Walker, and I laid back down for a bit, wondering about the kids and Jackson. My brain set the dream on repeat while I relived every moment in my mind.

* * *

I woke up Saturday morning feeling groggy. It was laundry day, and I gathered my clothes together. I walked them down the hall to the shared laundry room in my apartment building. I could hear my phone starting to ring from down the hall, so I rushed back in to answer.

"Hello?"

An unknown voice said my name, "Neil?" inquiring if it was me.

I said, "Yes." I wasn't prepared for this.

The voice said, "This is Jackson. Where are you?"

I laughed when I realized Walker had pranked me. He disguised his voice to perfection and quickly said, "Clubby." "Clubby" was a term we used to indicate we were going to the club or bar to cause a little trouble. That's what we do. That's all there was to do in Indianapolis.

I said, "Clubby," back and told him I'd see him at around 8:00. Then I did what most people do. I finished my laundry, watched TV, ate some dinner, and talked to a couple of other friends on the phone. I ended up taking a nap and wondered if I would pick up where I left off in that dream while I dozed off, but I didn't. Little did I know, that dream or vision still wasn't over.

I woke up with enough time to get ready to hang out with Walker. I wanted to look my best. As I finished, I realized it was pouring rain in large drops that night.

Chapter 8

The Escape

Sometime in the early '90s, I had purchased some albino tigersnake-skin Acme boots. Don't laugh. At the time, they were very expensive and all the rage. I really thought I was cool while wearing them, and they became kind of important on this night.

I arrived at Walker's house and went in for a drink. We both relaxed and had a few beers. I can't stress enough that Walker and I lived to mess with people. That's what the foundation of our friendship was, and that's what we always did. It may have been the only reason we even went out. After a few drinks, we decided to go to a local bar that had live music on weekends. Sometimes the bands were good, and other times they weren't so good.

Off we went, and we ended up at RAZZ-MA-TAZZ to invoke bewilderment on any and every one we could. One of the things I liked to do was watch people get up and walk from their table or the bar. If they left their drink behind, I would always go snag it and move it somewhere else. Watching patrons try to find their drink entertained me for hours. Walker was notorious for starting a tab and trying to leave without paying and had successfully accomplished that more than once.

All of this led up to the dream, yet again. All of this is about the dream.

Back to the bar and the snakeskin cowboy boots. We decided to leave and go to a hotel bar that wasn't far down the road. I was feeling the beers we had at the first place. As we arrived at the little hotel bar, we passed a couple of women coming out. I turned to Walker and said, "Dude, we got here too late."

Both women heard me, and one of them replied, "You're not too late. Let's go party."

I immediately turned and started walking with them. I asked where we were going and told them my name. We introduced ourselves and smiled. One said we were going to her place to have some wine. The other woman, who had been quiet up until now, said Walker couldn't come with us. I didn't realize at the time how lucky he was. I apologized to him and threw him my car keys. I told him to be careful. He laughed and replied, "Neil, 1. Walker, 0." I thought I was lucky, but when one messes with people like Walker and I did, sometimes you get a little karma. This was one of those nights.

We jumped in her car. She drove while her friend sat on my lap. When we pulled away, the rain started beating on the car. I kissed the girl who was sitting on my lap and had my hand on the driver's leg. Upon arriving to their apartment, we got out into the pouring rain. We ran to the apartment building where we had to walk up to the steps to the second floor. The whole time I was going up the steps, we were all talking, though I don't remember what the conversation was about. I'm sure it was meaningless party banter. I don't even remember them telling me their names. I had my arms around both of them.

As the driving woman went to unlock the door, she looked surprised. The door was unlocked already. We walked in, and I was kissing the woman who had sat on my lap. Now it was my turn to be surprised because two men were in the apartment. I was taken aback, and the driver said, "Hi honey," to one of them. She looked surprised to see him, and I don't think she was expecting him to be there. I don't remember those women's names, and I'm not sure I ever knew them. I was really drunk.

I do remember the events that happened next. The man said, "Who is this guy?"

I replied without letting them speak.

"I'm Neil, and these girls picked me up at the bar. We were going to have some fun." That wasn't very smart on my part, but I was being drunk honest. The girl who drove got angry and walked quickly to the phone. The men came over to confront me, and the other girl let go of my hand. I try to play it cool and say, "Look, I don't think they knew you were going to be here."

About that time, I overheard the girl on the phone say, "We don't know who he is. He followed us home from the bar, and he just walked into our apartment. He won't leave us alone."

I couldn't believe this was happening. I was supposed to be having fun with these women about now, and now it looked like I needed to get out of there alive and jail free. I started to explain to the man walking toward me now that she was lying. I realized it didn't matter what I said. He wasn't interested. So I adopted fight *and* flight. I stomped on his foot, pushed him to the floor, and ran out of the apartment as fast as I could. I ran down the stairs while hearing the man yelling for me to come back there, saying what he was going to do to me.

As I reached the bottom of the stairs, a police car pulled up with lights flashing. In the pouring rain, I heard, "Stop!"

He arrived fast. I imagined he was security for the complex. I didn't stop. It was pouring down rain with loud thunder and lightning striking all around. I was running through puddles in the parking lot, and my wonderful snakeskin cowboy boots were getting soaked. As I crossed the lot, the cop got back into his car and hit the spotlight. The chase was on.

I ran alongside a building out of the parking lot, and then around the back of the apartments. I reached a large fence that must have been at least eight feet tall, but I scaled it. I ran across a small creek in those snakeskin boots. As I looked back to the parking lot, all I could see was the spotlight sweeping the grounds and blue and red flashing lights, lighting up the entire rain-drenched sky. The whole front of the apartment complex lit up. I wondered how many police cars had shown up by this time.

As I ran past the creek, I came up to another fence just as tall as the first one. I scaled it as well and ran toward other apartments. The flashing lights behind me were fading, and I could finally catch my breath.

I wondered what I should do. I was being hunted like an escaped convict, and I did nothing wrong this time. I did realize how fast panic can sober a person.

I got up against another apartment building. I could see flashing lights traveling everywhere and guessed the storm kept the cops in their cars. I came across a few people sitting on their back porch cooking hot dogs on a grill and drinking beers under their porch. It was 2:00 in the morning on a Sunday, and it was storming. As I approached them, one of them asks, "Are you the one all of these cops are looking for?"

I admitted that I was, and they all laughed at me. I must have looked pathetic. I was soaking wet, muddy, out of breath, and my Acme $500 albino tigersnake cowboy boots were ruined.

They asked if I wanted a beer, and I accepted. After some introductions, I explained my situation to them. I told them everything from the kissing and the hand on the leg, to the men in the apartment and the phone call. I told them that the women claimed not to know me, saying I had just followed them into the apartment. All of it. I didn't hold back any details. One of the women on the back porch handed me a towel. They all laughed, and I couldn't help but join in.

As we sat on the porch, we had beer and hot dogs in the middle of a storm. We watched the police cars, spotlights, and flashing lights amidst the thunderstorm with a few laughs during moments of silence I spoke out, "Great start to the summer!" We laughed.

One said, "Here here!" and we all toasted a beer and chuckled, looking across the parking lot at the red and blue flashing lights on that wonderful summer night as a youth.

They told me I could stay the night, and I slept on the floor. I called Walker in the morning, asked how my car was, then said to come get me.

"You're not going to believe what happened."

"On my way," he replied after I gave him the directions.

Chapter 9
The Squirt Gun

A few months went by after the police chase. I felt like laying low was my best option. One Friday night, Walker called and said, "Clubby?" I repeated the word, but my tone was different. It felt like a curse word on my tongue, and I couldn't help but remember what had happened last time. Even so, I went with Walker. He had a surprise that night. He'd stopped by a Dollar General and found a tiny squirt gun the size of a big grape. He held it inside his hand while the nozzle stuck out just a little between his clenched fist. He showed me that it only shot once, about 15-20 feet, and then it had to be refilled. We were going to have a blast with that at the bar. Maybe pranks were just what I needed.

Evening came, and I drove to pick Walker up. We started with a drink at his place, as was our ritual, and then we were on our way. We went to a little sports pub where we could get a pitcher of beer, watch the race, and shoot some pool. That night, we sat at the bar. It was a square bar made of lacquered wood.

Nicks and scratches just made the surface look better in a place like this. The sides of the bar were about 15 feet long, and each side had a TV monitor above it. So no matter where we sat at the bar, we could watch whatever sporting event was playing.

We had a pitcher of beer and a NASCAR race on the TV. It was the night race, maybe Bristol, Tennessee. Every few minutes, cars were bumping into each other or getting into crashes. After watching the race for a while, we spotted an older gentleman spending his time just as we were, with beer and the race. He was yelling at the TV, obviously intoxicated. He was a stereotypical, loud-mouth drunk and kept on angrily interacting with the race. I figured he'd be the perfect selection for Walker's new toy. That would wait, though. *Let him have a few more drinks,* I thought. We decided to shoot a game of pool, and we played it strictly to mess with anyone who wanted to eavesdrop. We usually tried to entice people to do so by yelling out strange things while playing, so no one knew just what kind of pool game we were playing. For instance, we would say "two" or fractions like "two and five thirds" before every shot.

After several shots a piece of saying these kinds of numbers loudly, nearby pool players started watching us and asking questions. It was all in good fun, and we always enjoyed making up different stories for every question. On this particular night, Walker grabbed the cue ball and held it up. He said, "Hey, Neil, Pearl!" as if the cue ball was a giant pearl. That summoned the memory of the scorched children from the dream. The old man came to mind, too. Were they still waiting for me?

Even though several months had passed since the dream or vision, it still weighed heavily on my mind. I could still see the people clearly and remember all the details and events I experienced while in that place. Walker knew this, obviously, and had fun with it from time to time. I still couldn't help but think I had let them down, the children and Jackson. They all told me over and over not to forget them. They knew I would help and said I should hurry back. I thought about it too much. Why did they think I would help? And how could I if I didn't know how? Or where were they? It was just some kind of hallucination or vivid dream that I let get the better of me. I tried not to think about the dream, but I rarely succeeded. It's disappointing to me, and I think about it often enough.

After our fun with the yelling of all kinds of numbers with fractions and confusing all the other pool players nearby, we went back to the bar. The old drunk man was still yelling about the race and everything else. Now was the time to try out the new toy on this guy. Walker and I were quite drunk by now, and he went to the bathroom to fill up the squirt gun. This old man was sitting diagonally from us, around 12-14 feet away. No one was sitting next to him or behind him, unsurprising with how loud he was.

Walker came back with a huge grin on his face. He plopped down on his seat and fired the squirt gun right at the old man's face without even looking at him. No one would have known it was him because of how small the toy was. It hit the drunk man right on the side of his face, and he immediately yelled, "Hey! Someone threw water at me!"

Walker and I couldn't help but laugh but watched the TV, so the man wouldn't think we were laughing at him. We didn't even look at him even though he was still barking his words loudly while wiping the water off his face.

The attractive female bartender gave the old man a scowl and asked if he was okay. The man told her what had happened. She must have thought he was just a drunk man who was living outside reality because she just shrugged him off and walked away. As she walked away, she said, "Well, you need to turn your volume down. You're getting a little loud."

Walker looked at me, smiling, and slid the squirt gun to me and said, "Your turn."

I was laughing again already, just thinking about using it on this loud, drunk man. While I was in the bathroom to fill it up, I took a practice shot. The little squirt gun shot far enough to surprise me. As I walked out, I couldn't stop grinning, and neither could Walker. I sat down on my stool at the bar next to Walker. I held tight onto the squirt gun and waited… and waited…

…and *bam!* I pushed the trigger. No one noticed anything except the drunk man. I got him in the ear, neck, and part of the back of his head. This time, he stood up and yelled, almost knocking the barstool next to him over.

"Someone is throwing water on me!"

Walker and I turned back to the TV, laughing and pretending we didn't see the man who was yelling obscenities. By this time, the bartender confronted him and said, "That's enough. You need to stop cursing and yelling. After you finish that beer, it might be time for you to go."

The bouncer was standing by her side, so he knew how serious she was. He started to plead his innocence and explained what was happening, his words slurring. They must have thought he was crazy because no one was near him. We were more than 10 feet away from him, so we couldn't be doing it. We weren't even looking at him. Walker even asked the bartender what the man's problem was. We tried to look annoyed, like he was disturbing our beer and NASCAR time. She shrugged her shoulders and said, "He's just drunk. Don't pay attention to him."

I answered her and said, "Well, we are all trying to watch the race and have a good time. It looks like that drunkard is trying to cause trouble."

She apologized and walked away. Walker and I glanced at each other and laughed again. I slid the squirt gun back to him, so he could take the next shot. He laughed and said, "This one should push him over the edge."

He was getting ready to go to the bathroom to refill the toy when I noticed someone at a table next to us had gotten up, leaving his drink behind. I was watching him and talking to Walker, all while observing the drink. The man grabbed his cigarettes from his pocket and walked to the door to smoke outside. Walker got up to head to the bathroom. Shortly after that, I got up and grabbed the man's drink. I walked to the jukebox and dropped it in the trash next to it. It looked like a mixed drunk, maybe a 7 and 7. I decided to check out the music selection on the jukebox, laughing for a moment before making my way back to my seat. I couldn't swipe the grin off my face at the knowledge and anticipation that we would be pranking two people at the same time.

Walker came back, just as giddy as I was. He sat for a moment, waiting for his chance. The drunk man was even worse off than before, and I could tell the bartender is aggravated by his mere presence. Then Walker took his shot. The water went right into the man's ear again. I couldn't believe how well this was working, and no one had noticed anything. The drunk man jumped up, yelling at the top of his lungs and knocking down two barstools in the process.

"Someone is throwing water on me!" He was cursing and throwing his arms around in the air as if trying to hit someone. No one was near him, so he just looked like a crazy person. We were laughing again and pointing at the TV, pretending we were distracted.

The bartender rushed toward the old man and told him to settle down. He once again pleaded his case, but she wouldn't listen to him. She said he needed to leave. Walker decided to poke the bear and shouted, "Yo! What's your problem, you drunk?"

The man just got crazier and more animated. She picked up her walkie talkie and asked for the bouncer to escort the drunk man out of the bar. He wasn't going to leave quietly and said, "I'm not leaving."

The man with the cigarettes came back in from his smoking break and asked loudly, "Where's my drink?"

Walker knew right away that this was my work. He turned to me, laughed, and said, "Good one, dude."

By now we had an old drunk man, who was now fighting the bouncer and being dragged out of the bar, and the man with the missing drink, who was now yelling at the bartender about how we wasn't done with his drink.

"As a matter of fact, it was nearly full. Who took it and why?"

She stood her ground and told him she didn't take his drink, but he challenged her, demanding a new drink. She wasn't in the mood and went right back to the walkie talkie.

"Can you come remove another loud drunk?"

We were laughing the whole time while pretending to watch the TV.

When the excitement died down, Walker turned to the bartender and said, "Man, we came here to watch the race in peace, but this place is kind of rowdy. There must be a lot of fights in here."

She shook her head and said, "No, not usually. Must be something in the air tonight."

Walker and I laughed.

Chapter 10
Revelation

A few more months had passed, and we shared many more nights of pranks at the bars. My mind always went back to that dream or vision or whatever it was. Maybe it was a dream like the ones men had in Biblical times, like Joseph and others before the magic of technology and geo-engineering and Haarp and who knows what else. Maybe that's how everyone used to dream, and for some reason, that particular night, I found that place. Throughout all the time that had passed from the night of the dream to the years it has now been, I have remembered it like a real memory, down to the last little details. My memory was like a story book that I could just pull from the shelf, glance over, and remember everything all over again.

Long ago, dreams were important and almost always had a deeper meaning. Dream interpreters had a valued service to offer society long ago. What happened? Did dreams just all the sudden become random, meaningless pictures of distorted thoughts? And if so, why? When did this happen? So few speak of this anymore. I suppose all those questions are for another time and a bit of research for another book.

I'm just trying to convey the type of dream I had as well as speculate what kind of dream it was to satisfy my own mind. But they used to happen all the time and were widely accepted as fact. Supernatural dreams were real and needed interpretation. Joseph with his coat of many colors once interpreted dreams for a king. He himself became the king's right-hand man. If you had the gift of interpretation, you could rule and save half of the known world. Joseph saved so many people with his interpretation of the king's dream about the seven years of plenty and seven years of drought and his subsequent plan to save in the years of plenty.

Why do dreams mean nothing now? I knew this dream meant something, like ones of old, and I was about to find out how.

It was Saint Patrick's Day evening at the time of my revelation. Walker and I were in downtown Indianapolis, celebrating the tradition with green beer. The canal was green, people were wearing green, and at some point, most of us ended up peeing in green. After a few green beers, we just couldn't help it. We were pulling our usual tricks on people, exchanging pleasantries with strangers, meeting new people, and so on. While coming out of one bar, we noticed a big crane parked outside one of the larger bars. We decided to wade through the sea of green people toward that crane. As we approached, we could see that there was a short line next to crane of brave and idiotic people willing to pay money to bungee jump from it.

It was entertaining to converse with the lovely women outside while drinking our green beer and watching the brave at heart jump. The crane would actually lower a cable in which a small box big enough for two would take you to a platform near the top. The instructor stood with each person, making sure everything was secure, and watched him or her leap.

While Walker and I were out there watching, I noticed two beautiful young ladies standing nearby watching with drinks in their hands. We moved closer to them in hopes of striking up a conversation. We stood closer but weren't ready to make conversation yet. I wanted to be smooth, so I could impress these beautiful women. I said to Walker loudly enough for the women to hear, "I would jump if I didn't want to throw away 50 bucks."

They heard, which turned out to be good and bad. The good was that they moved closer and introduced themselves as Jenna and Sarah. They were sisters. We introduced ourselves, and Sarah said, "I couldn't help but overhear you saying you would jump if you had 50 to waste?"

"Yeah," I replied.

They started laughing. I had just been showing off and trying to look manly. I was usually good at showing off, but I had a habit of looking foolish. This night did not disappoint.

I decided to dig my heels in and said, "Yeah, that's right."

Walker tried to help me out like the best friend he was and asked where the women were from. Sarah was the one to respond again.

"My sister is from here, but I'm up from Jackson, Mississippi, to go to her wedding." We were disappointed that one was getting married.

After making small talk with them for a while and watching a few jumpers, I couldn't help but wonder about the people jumping. They were so high, and they couldn't be sure of the security of the ropes. I wondered how they felt as they got closer to the edge and if they could actually enjoy it. How many beers does it take to jump off a crane? How did the air feel as they fell? And what did the jolt and pull back up do to their nerves?

Sarah broke my concentration when she said, "I'll buy your ticket if you jump."

I couldn't believe my ears. I was just trying to show off and didn't want to jump. I was drunk and wanted to talk to pretty ladies, not put my life at risk. Walker could sense my hesitation and egged me on.

"Yeah, you said you wanted to jump, dude," he said, laughing.

I wanted to kill him, but these beautiful women were calling me out and offering to pay for me to jump. This was my chance, and I was going to suck it up and jump. I couldn't back out and be called a wimp.

After a few laughs and another green beer for each of us, we went to get my ticket. Walker couldn't look at me without chuckling. He'd been a witness to me putting my foot in my mouth on more than one occasion. My little crowd was cheering me on as I rode up a small elevator to the top of the crane. The instructor could tell I was scared to death. Walker, Sarah, and Jenna were shrinking as I ascended into the sky, but I could hear them cheering me on.

Reality hit me like a ton of bricks, jolting me like a thunderbolt. My mind was racing at one thought, a revelation. Sarah was from Jackson, and she bought my ticket. If this led to my death, maybe my end was from Jackson. My mind went back to that dream.

I was standing at the top platform getting strapped into the harness that wrapped me up like cobwebs. People were cheering for me below, but they felt so distant. I could hear music playing all around me, but the wind that blew around me dulled the sound. Now all I could think of was the woman from Jackson. I heard a countdown from five begin, but I didn't wait until I heard the one. I just went for it and walked off the platform. I felt a rush hit me as the cool air pulled my hair back. The woman said she was from Jackson, almost like the old man sent her to me. My stomach turned. No amount of liquid courage could have prepared me for this. I reached the bottom of the line and jolted back up. The liquid courage was going to come up. And then it did. Twice. Silence stunned the crowd as they tried to figure out where it was safe to stand. Green beer vomit rained down. I was so embarrassed, but that's what I got for running my mouth again.

I got down to the ground and was unstrapped. My friends were laughing at me, and they made fun of my little adventure. We all talked through a few more beers and then parted ways. The entire rest of the night, I was thinking of Jackson, sent by Jackson, from Jackson. I knew now that I had to look at a map to find those kids who cried out to me in that dream. And there was no better place to start than in Jackson, Mississippi.

Chapter 11
Atlas

I worked in construction for a long time. At the time, I would go to different grocery stores and indulge in the 50 cent or dollar toys in the machines in the entrance, the ones in the plastic balls with the removable lid. I didn't care about the toy; I just wanted the empty ball. That might sound strange for an adult man to do, but I kept a few in my glovebox of my work truck. On certain jobs when I would inspect footings on big buildings, I would write my name and date on a piece of paper and put it inside the empty ball. Then I would bury it next to a corner of the foundation. I did this because I could imagine someday long into the future, archeologists might be digging and find ruins of an old wall, then find my little plastic ball with my name and date in it.

As time went on, they might find more and more of these plastic balls, always next to ruins or thick stone concrete, buildings, or footings. Maybe they might think I was important in the distant past, or that I was present every time something was built or destroyed. Either way, there could be all kinds of scenarios that would involve me that they would speculate about, and they would know of me when they opened that plastic ball.

While I lay in bed one night chuckling about that, I realized I even liked playing pranks on people long into the future. I couldn't help but think maybe somehow that's what those children did in that dream. Maybe they left a little bit of themselves somewhere, and if conditions were right, someone would eventually find them.

Several days passed. I had told Walker about that dream many times by now, and he was familiar with every little detail. Maybe I talked about it so much because I was afraid to forget it, though I can't imagine forgetting anything about it. He was helping me along the way, trying to unravel its meaning. With it being supernatural to me, I needed all the help I could get. So I called Walker and told him we should get a road map atlas to look up Jackson, Mississippi. He said, "It's about time. I'm a little busy now, but I'll be over in a few hours."

I waited for him to arrive, my mind running through all the different scenarios of what I might find or not find. Was I crazy? What if I find something? What if I find nothing? Should I even look? Maybe I should let it rest and leave it be.

I remember in school we had to memorize all the state capitals, and I knew Jackson was Mississippi's capital. I hadn't thought of that before since I hadn't even been to Mississippi. I also never considered a person's name in a dream could indicate a location. I knew nothing of dreams, and I don't know much about them now even, except that they can have meaning. They were seen as important at some point in history, stopped being as important or valued, and started being meaningless. How are dreams so precious at one time but not today? Now people assume dreams are about the sleeping person's anxiety or forgetfulness. The scale is completely different. This was so puzzling to me now. When did they change to nothing?

I was lost in thought, my mind racing with what dreams once were and what they have become when Walker knocked at my door and yelled through, "Jackson's here!"

Rain was pelting the building, and Walker's clothes had drops all over them. He came in, and we talked about the next step if we did find something. We didn't know what to do. I suggested we find the map and see if we could find a town or anything called Pearl near Jackson. So off we went down to the old blue and white truck stop not far from my parents' house off of I-74. As a child, I rode my bike there with my neighborhood friends, and we would all get breakfast.

I wanted to stop by my elderly parents' house on the way to check on them. They often needed me to help them around the house to cut the grass, pick up branches, load the burn pile, and so on. I figured I would kill two birds with one stone by going to that truck stop as well.

When we arrived, we went straight to the shopping area for truckers. They had shelves and racks filled with DVDs, stereos, snacks, drinks, but very few maps. I'm an old guy and prefer a paper map that I can hold in my hand and spread out across the table. Walker said he was hungry, so we both ordered French toast and coffee from the attached diner. I went to grab the Rand McNally Road Atlas and brought it back to our table. We spread it out and turn to the Mississippi page and immediately see Jackson.

Don't forget us.

We will be waiting.

I promise I will get help and be back.

I remembered clearly the kids and Jackson's words running through my mind, and it just motivated me to find answers. I could still see all three of them standing near that old slab and the cellar doors up on the bank, waving at me. I remember it so clearly. What was I going to find? Then as I sat there lost in my thoughts, I heard the words, "There it is!"

Walker found it! He found Pearl. It's a real place just a few miles east of Jackson, and Jackson led us to it.

I'm a simple working-class man. I've never been to Mississippi or even given a trip there a thought. I'd certainly never heard of this small town of Pearl. We continued to look over the map, and I specifically looked for that winding country road from my dream. It was in the middle of nowhere with a large creek or small river running alongside it from time to time.

The whole time I was looking for familiar roads, Walker was shocked. He said, "Dude, you had a supernatural experience! Now I bet there are spirits waiting on you to be laid to rest." He went on and on about this and that and the deeper meanings to all of this. I was more than a little scared. I was curious and terrified. I didn't have many resources or much money, so I couldn't just take off and go to Pearl. I wouldn't know what to do if I was able to. I would probably lose my job and then be homeless. If I told anyone else, they would think I was crazy or that I made it up. I had all these reasons to run, to hide my dream and try to live my life distracted from that night. But this dream or vision happened, and it was sent to me in Indiana. How could I not try to do *something?* I promised.

The more I looked at the map, the one thing I noticed was the roads to the south of Pearl. They looked more familiar; the openness of the country and all the winding roads. I remembered that I hadn't seen a house or building the whole time I was driving that orange Mustang. I kept seeing that waterway on my right, which meant I was driving west or south, or southwest.

I couldn't find a detailed map of the land around Pearl. The landmarks I thought might be on the map weren't there. The roads looked more the way I pictured in my mind to the south, to a small town called Pearl River. Maybe that's why Jackson had me get in the canoe. If I could just understand, I could find them. Maybe the old green and white, aged sign on the side of the bank was a metaphor for Pearl River.

We studied the map over our breakfast, and I thought of all the possibilities. One thing was for sure: If part of the dream was proven to be real, then what about those kids? In my mind, it was all true. Somewhere there in Pear or Pearl River, there were spirits of those little burnt children, hidden by time and overgrowth, forgotten by loved ones and the community. The authorities had missed them, but they found me. To get to them and to help them would take money, time, and some investigation. I don't know the children's names. I don't know where their parents are. I don't know if the kids were murdered or accidentally killed. I did know that Jackson and Pearl were real. I only hoped that someone else had found the concrete slab by now and the bodies in the cellar. The children need to be laid to rest.

Walker and I decided to take a week off for a trip next year. We'll drive around in the areas around Pearl and look for the remnants of the house. I wish I could rent an old, orange '66 convertible Mustang to drive along the way. Maybe, if we're close, the kids will come out into the road again and flag us down. I can picture the old man, Jackson, standing there hand in hand with them, smiling at me. They know I won't abandon them, and I want to hug the kids again. Wherever they are, I hope Jackson is with them. I'm sure he still checks up on them from time to time. I miss them, and I want to tell them I love them. I want to tell them I didn't forget and show them this book. Lastly, I want to tell them that Walker and I are coming!

This book is my way to help them. It is all I could offer. I made a promise, and a promise is a promise.

Walker said something disturbing to me upon completing this book. He said, "When word gets out about this book, and it will, what will you do when more reach out? Are you prepared for more visions?"

I stared blankly ahead. I heard birds singing; I smelled the fresh blossomed flowers of spring and rain. I felt the warm breeze and sun against my skin. I saw the trees swaying in the wind.

THE END